C is for Confusion...

"One of us should run to the police station now," Dink said.

Suddenly three things happened at once: The upstairs light blazed on. Dink heard a loud scream. And a police whistle blared through the open window.

Dink leaped to his feet. Mrs. Davis was up there, and so was the burglar!

But which one had let out that scream?

The A to Z Mysteries™ series!

The Absent Author

The Bald Bandit

The Canary Caper

The Deadly Dungeon

For Sarah
—R.R.

To Matthew for being a great Josh
—J.C.

Text copyright © 1998 by Ron Roy.
Illustrations copyright © 1998 by John Steven Gurney.
All rights reserved under International and Pan-American Copyright Conventions.
Published in the United States by Random House, Inc., New York, and simultaneously in Canada by Random House of Canada Limited, Toronto.

http://www.randomhouse.com/

Library of Congress Cataloging-in-Publication Data
Roy, Ron, 1940–
The canary caper / by Ron Roy ; illustrated by John Steven Gurney.
p.   cm. — (A to Z mysteries)
"A stepping stone book."
SUMMARY: Dink and his friends investigate why pets, like Mrs. Davis's canary, Mozart, are mysteriously disappearing all over town.
ISBN 0-679-88593-5 (pbk.) — ISBN 0-679-98593-X (lib. bdg.)
[1. Pets—Fiction. 2. Lost and found possessions—Fiction. 3. Mystery and detective stories.] I. Gurney, John, ill. II. Title. III. Series: Roy, Ron, 1940– A to Z mysteries.
PZ7.R8139Can 1997 [E]—dc21 97-15564

Printed in the United States of America   40 39 38 37

A to Z Mysteries™

The Canary Caper

by **Ron Roy**

illustrated by
John Steven Gurney

A STEPPING STONE BOOK™

Random House New York

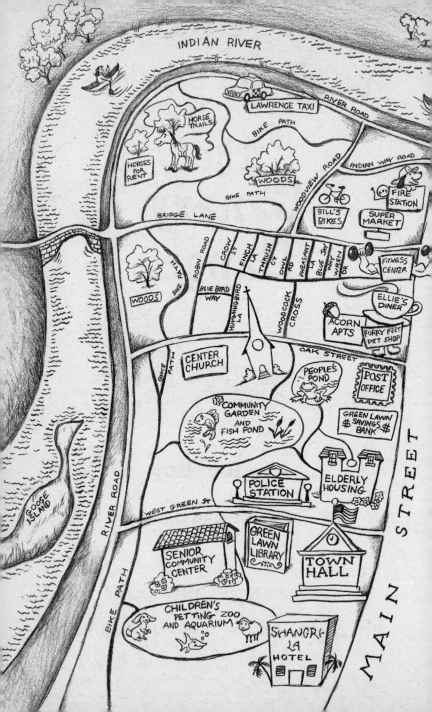

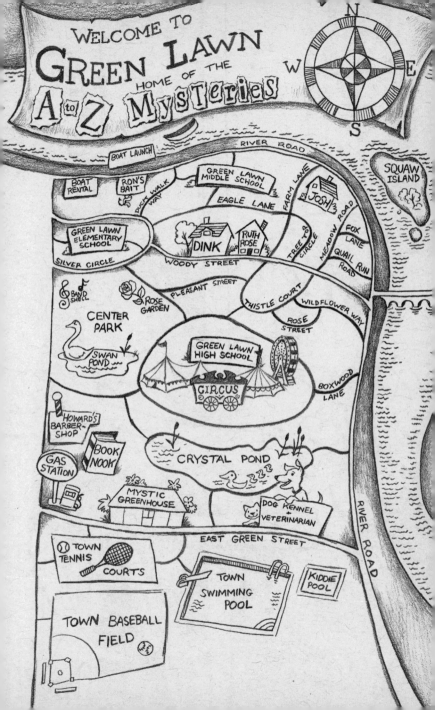

Chapter 1

Dink Duncan opened his front door. His best friend, Josh Pinto, was standing on the steps. "Hi, Josh. C'mon in," said Dink. "I just finished lunch."

Josh hurried past Dink, wiping his forehead. "We sure picked the hottest day of the summer to go to the circus," he said. "I just took a shower, and I'm still hot."

Dink grinned. "You took a shower? Let's see, that's two showers this month, right?"

"Haw haw, very funny," Josh said. He opened the refrigerator door and pulled up his shirt. "Ahh, that feels good!"

"It won't feel so good if my mom catches you," Dink said.

Josh grabbed the apple juice and flopped into a chair. "You're funny, but it's too hot to laugh," he said, pouring himself a glass. "Where's Ruth Rose? It's almost time to leave."

"She's waiting next door." Dink put his plate in the sink. "I have to run up and brush my teeth."

"Forget your teeth—the circus is waiting!"

Dink grinned and pointed to a clown-faced cookie jar on the counter. "Grab a cookie. I'll be right down."

Josh made a beeline for the cookie jar. "Take your time brushing," he said.

"Don't eat all of them!" Dink said, leaping up the stairs.

"Dink," his mother called, "are you running?"

"Sorry, Mom," he called back. "We're in a hurry. Thursday is half-price admission if we get to the circus by one o'clock."

Dink brushed his teeth, yanked a comb through his blond hair, then charged back down the stairs.

"Donald David Duncan!" his mother yelled. "No running in the house!"

The phone rang in the kitchen.

"Got it, Mom!" Dink grabbed the phone, watching Josh stuff a whole cookie into his mouth. "Hello, Duncan residence."

Dink listened, then said, "We'll be over in five minutes." He hung up.

"We'll be over where in five minutes?" Josh asked.

"Mrs. Davis's house. You know her canary, Mozart? He's escaped."

"What about the circus?" asked Josh. "Half-price, remember?"

Dink shrugged. "So we pay full price. Mrs. Davis needs our help."

They walked next door to Ruth Rose's house and rang the bell. Four-year-old Nate Hathaway opened the door. He stared up at Dink with huge blue eyes.

"Hi, Natie," said Dink. "Is Ruth Rose ready?"

Nate's lips, cheeks, and T-shirt were smeared with chocolate. He was holding a raggedy stuffed dinosaur.

"Sheef ungt fruz," Nate said with a full mouth.

Dink laughed. "She's *what?*"

Ruth Rose showed up behind Nate.

"MOM, WE'RE LEAVING NOW!" she screamed into the house.

Josh clapped both hands over his ears. "Ruth Rose, you should get a job as a car salesman. Then you could yell all day and get paid for it."

Ruth Rose stepped outside and closed the door. "You know perfectly well that I'm going to be President," she said sweetly. "And it's sales*woman*, Josh."

Ruth Rose liked to dress in one color. Today it was purple, from her sneakers to the headband holding back her black curls.

While they walked down Woody Street, Dink told Ruth Rose about Mrs. Davis's missing canary.

"Mozart got out of his cage?" Ruth Rose said. "I hope he doesn't fly over here. Tiger could swallow a canary in one bite."

"Your fat cat could swallow a turkey in one bite," Josh said.

Ruth Rose rolled her eyes. "Tiger is plump," she said, "not fat. Race you!"

Mrs. Davis was standing in the doorway of her large yellow house when they arrived. "Thank you for coming right over," she said.

Mrs. Davis held a handkerchief, and her eyes were red. "I didn't know who else to call."

"We don't mind," Dink said. "What happened to Mozart?"

"After breakfast, I hung his cage out back so he could have some fresh air. But when I went to give him his lunch, his cage was empty!"

"I'm sure he's somewhere nearby. Don't worry!" Dink said.

Dink, Josh, and Ruth Rose ran around to the backyard. Mozart's cage was hanging in an apple tree.

"Split up," Dink said. "Check all the bushes and flowers."

The kids searched every tree, shrub, and flower bed. Mrs. Davis watched from her back porch. "Any luck?" she asked Dink.

He shook his head. "I'm afraid not, but we'll keep looking."

"It's such a beautiful day," Mrs. Davis said. "I hope you kids have something fun planned."

"After we find Mozart, we're going to the circus," Dink told her.

"The circus! Well, please don't let me stop you!" Mrs. Davis said. "Mozart knows his cage. I'm sure he'll fly home soon."

But Dink could tell that Mrs. Davis wasn't really so sure. "Okay, but we'll call you later," he promised.

They said good-bye to Mrs. Davis and headed for the high school. The

Tinker Town Traveling Circus had set up on the school baseball field the day before and would leave town Monday night.

The kids cut through a bunch of circus trailers and trucks on their way to the admissions gate. The sides of the trailers were painted with pictures of clowns, tigers, and elephants.

They arrived five minutes after one, but the ticket lady let them in for half-price anyway, a dollar each.

"What'll we do first?" Ruth Rose asked.

"Let's eat," Josh said.

"No way," Dink said. "You already had lunch, and you probably gobbled down half my mom's cookies. Let's walk around and see what's here."

They watched birds do tricks, dogs ride on ponies, and a chimp dressed like Elvis "sing" into a microphone.

They all gulped when a tiger trainer put his hand right inside a tiger's mouth.

"Guess the tiger's not hungry," Josh said with a grin.

In Clown Corner, a clown dressed as a giraffe danced on stilts. He kept time to the music by snapping his yellow suspenders.

"I have to leave soon," Ruth Rose

said after a while. "My mom needs me to watch Nate while she goes shopping."

The kids left, cutting through the town rose garden to get to Woody Street.

Dink snapped his fingers. "I just remembered—my mom said I can set up my tent in the backyard. Can you guys get permission to sleep out?"

"No problem for me," Josh said.

"Nate's never slept in a tent, so I'll bring him," Ruth Rose said. "And Tiger," she added sweetly.

"Your little brother!" Josh yelped. "Great, we'll have our own circus—a four-year-old monkey and a man-eating tiger!"

Ruth Rose laughed. "Don't worry. We'll bring our own tent."

Dink and Josh dropped Ruth Rose off at her house, then continued on to

Dink's. There they went inside and called Mrs. Davis.

"She says Mozart hasn't come back," Dink told Josh after he'd hung up.

While they were pitching Dink's tent, Ruth Rose came over. Nate trailed behind her, dragging his extinct-looking stuffed dinosaur.

"Hey, where's your man-eating cat?" Josh asked.

Ruth Rose dropped her tent on the ground. She looked as if she'd just swallowed something nasty.

"What's the matter, Ruth Rose?" Dink asked.

"Tiger is missing," Ruth Rose said quietly. "And my mother says she hasn't been home all day."

Chapter 2

Early the next morning, Ruth Rose poked her head into Dink's tent. "Wake up, you guys!"

Dink shot up out of a sound sleep. "Did Tiger come back?" he asked, peering sleepily at Ruth Rose.

"No, she didn't. I'm going to the police station and I want you guys to come with me."

Josh rolled over in his sleeping bag. "To report a missing cat?"

"No, to report a missing cat *and* a missing canary," Ruth Rose said. Then she ducked back out of the tent.

Dink and Josh looked at each other, then crawled out after her. Ruth Rose was pacing back and forth across the lawn.

"Guys, it's just too weird," she said. "Two animals disappeared from the same street on the same day!" Ruth Rose stopped pacing and looked at them. "I don't think Mozart and Tiger wandered off, I think they were stolen. I'm taking Nate home, and then you guys are coming with me to talk to Officer Fallon."

Ruth Rose woke up Nate, took his hand, and marched toward her house.

Dink and Josh just looked at each other and shrugged. Then they walked into Dink's house. Josh poured two bowls of cereal while Dink ran up to his room to change. Loretta, his guinea pig, squeaked a hello to Dink from her cage.

Josh was slurping up his Weet Treets when Dink came back down.

"I've been thinking," Josh said. "Wouldn't Tiger eat Mozart if someone kidnapped them both?"

Dink shrugged. "I don't know. I'm not even sure that Tiger and Mozart were kidnapped," he said between bites. "But Ruth Rose is our friend, so let's go to the police station with her."

Ruth Rose walked in wearing blue shorts and a red shirt. "You guys ready to go?" she asked.

Dink stared. He'd never seen Ruth Rose wear two different colors at the same time. He gave Josh a look, but Josh was busy reading the back of the cereal box and didn't notice.

"Yup, we're ready," Dink said, putting the bowls and glasses in the sink.

They found Officer Fallon at his desk. He was typing at his computer, chewing gum, and sipping tea all at the same time.

"Well, hi, gang," he said, smiling at the kids. "Going to the circus this weekend? How about some free passes?"

"No thanks, we went yesterday," Dink said.

Officer Fallon handed Josh three tickets. "Go again, on the Green Lawn Police!"

"Officer Fallon, I have a problem," Ruth Rose said.

He pointed at some chairs. "Have a seat. I'm all ears."

"It's my cat, Tiger. She's been gone for a whole day and night," Ruth Rose said. "She's never been away from home that long! Mrs. Davis's canary disappeared, too!"

Dink had never seen Ruth Rose look or sound so serious.

Officer Fallon wrote something on a sheet of paper.

"I think someone in Green Lawn is stealing pets," Ruth Rose went on. "Two pets vanishing on the same day is just too weird!"

"Four pets," Officer Fallon said. He opened his drawer and pulled out a sheet of paper. "Four pets are missing."

"Four?" Dink and Josh said together.

Officer Fallon nodded. "Last night, Dr. Pardue called. His kids' rabbit was missing from its cage. Later, Mrs. Gwynn called. It seems her parrot disappeared off her back porch."

"All yesterday?" Dink asked.

Officer Fallon nodded.

"I was right!" Ruth Rose said, jumping to her feet. "There *is* a pet-napper around here!"

"Four animals disappearing on the same day does seem strange," Officer Fallon said. "In fact, I've already asked Officer Keene to look into it."

He looked at Ruth Rose. "Could it be that your cat just took a little vacation, Ruth Rose? I used to have a cat who was a real wanderer."

"Well, Tiger isn't," Ruth Rose answered firmly.

Officer Fallon nodded. He told the kids he'd let them know if he discovered anything.

The kids left the police station and walked toward Main Street.

"Sounds like you might be right, Ruth Rose," Dink said.

"Maybe we should go see Mrs. Wong, just in case," Josh suggested. "People always bring her stray animals. Maybe someone found Tiger and brought her to the pet shop."

Ruth Rose rewarded Josh with a huge smile. "Great idea, Josh!"

They passed Howard's Barbershop. Howard was out front, sweeping his sidewalk.

"Have you seen my big orange cat?" Ruth Rose called.

Howard shook his head. "Sorry, Ruth Rose."

At the Furry Feet pet shop, Mrs.

Wong told Ruth Rose the same thing. "Nobody brought Tiger in," she said. "But I'll keep my eyes peeled."

"Mrs. Davis's canary is gone, too," Dink told Mrs. Wong.

"And Dr. Pardue's rabbit and Mrs. Gwynn's parrot!" Josh said.

"Four animals are missing? That *is* very strange!" Mrs. Wong glanced around her shop. "I guess I should count my own critters!"

"May I use your phone, Mrs. Wong?" Ruth Rose asked. "I want to call my mom and see if Tiger's home yet."

"Help yourself," Mrs. Wong said.

Ruth Rose dialed, spoke quietly to her mother, then hung up.

"Tiger's still gone," she said. "Who'd want to steal a canary, a cat, a parrot, and a rabbit?"

"I don't know," Dink said. "But we're going to find out!"

Chapter 3

The kids left the pet shop and headed up Main Street. They walked slowly, thinking about what to do.

"I've read about scientists stealing animals to use in experiments," Josh said.

"That's awful!" Dink said.

"I don't want Tiger used in some

experiment!" said Ruth Rose. "We have to find those animals. Where do the Gwynns and the Pardues live?"

"The Gwynns live over by us, on Thistle Court," Dink said.

"Why don't we go talk to them?" Ruth Rose said. "Maybe the pet-napper left some clues."

The kids cut through the high school grounds and passed the circus trailers. A few of the workers were sitting at a picnic table drinking coffee. They waved when the kids walked by.

"Which house is the Gwynns'?" Ruth Rose asked when they reached Thistle Court.

"That big gray one," Josh said. The mailbox in front said GWYNN in black letters.

Ruth Rose walked up the steps and rang the doorbell. Mrs. Gwynn opened the door.

"Hi, kids! How's your summer so far?" she asked.

"Not so great," Ruth Rose said. "Someone stole my cat yesterday."

"Oh, Ruth Rose, how awful! My parrot disappeared yesterday, too!"

"So did Mrs. Davis's canary," Josh added.

"We just came from the police station," Dink put in. "Officer Fallon told us about your parrot. Dr. Pardue's rabbit is also missing."

Mrs. Gwynn's mouth fell open. "My goodness! Do you mean that four pets disappeared yesterday?"

"We think so," Ruth Rose said. "Where was your parrot when you last saw him?"

"On my back porch, in his cage," Mrs. Gwynn said.

"Can we see the cage?" Dink asked.

Mrs. Gwynn took them through the

kitchen to a screened-in back porch. A cage stood in one corner.

"Archie likes it out here," said Mrs. Gwynn. "He can watch the other birds in the trees. Yesterday I came out to have my lunch, but he was gone."

Dink checked the screen door that led to the backyard. "Was this locked?" he asked.

"I don't really remember. We often leave it unlocked," Mrs. Gwynn said.

"Could Archie have opened his cage door himself?" Josh asked.

Mrs. Gwynn shook her head. "We always keep a clothespin on his door to make sure he can't open it."

"So someone must have stolen him," Ruth Rose said.

"Oh, dear, I don't like to think of crime in Green Lawn," Mrs. Gwynn said with a sigh. "Can I offer you kids something to drink? It's pretty warm."

"No thanks," Ruth Rose said. "But do you mind if we look in your phone book for Dr. Pardue's address?"

"They're at number three Pheasant Lane," Mrs. Gwynn said. "I drop Mike off there to play tennis with Andy Pardue."

The kids thanked Mrs. Gwynn and hurried to Main Street.

"This is getting weirder and weirder," Dink said. "A canary and a parrot were snatched right out of their cages in broad daylight. With people home!"

"And Tiger was probably in my backyard when she was taken," Ruth Rose said.

They waved to Mr. Paskey at the Book Nook and headed up Aviary Way. Three Pheasant Lane was a big green house surrounded by tall trees. A kid holding a tennis racket was sitting on the front porch.

"Hi," Ruth Rose said, walking up to the porch. "Is Dr. Pardue home? We'd like to talk to him about his rabbit."

"I'm Andy Pardue," the kid said. "Violet's my rabbit. Why? Did you find her?"

"No, but my cat is missing, too," Ruth Rose said. "And so are two other pets in town."

Dink glanced around the Pardues' front yard. "When did your rabbit disappear?" he asked Andy.

"After lunch yesterday," he said. "My sister ran into the house screaming. I went out to the cage, and the door was wide open. Violet was gone."

"Can you show us the cage?" Ruth Rose asked.

Andy led them to the backyard. An empty rabbit hutch stood under a tree.

"Was the cage locked?" Josh asked.

"Yep, I lock it every night myself."

Andy Pardue gave them a sharp look. "What's going on, anyway? A ring of animal thieves?"

"That's what we're trying to find out," Dink said.

"Well, let me know what you dig up," said Andy. "Boy, I'd like to get my hands on the creep who did this. My little sister cried all night!"

The kids walked back to Woody Street.

"Let's stop and check in with Mrs. Davis," Dink suggested as they passed her house. "We should tell her about the other missing animals."

When Mrs. Davis opened her door, she had a big smile on her face.

"Oh, I'm so glad to see you three!" she exclaimed. "You'll never guess! A man just called. He said he found Mozart! He's bringing him here at six-thirty. Isn't that lovely?"

"That's great." Dink looked at Josh and Ruth Rose in surprise.

"I want you three to be here, since you were kind enough to look for him," Mrs. Davis continued. "Afterward, we'll have some of my strawberry shortcake to celebrate!"

"Super!" Josh said.

"We'll see you at six-thirty," Dink said with a wave.

The three started home.

Josh grinned. "I guess Mozart wasn't kidnapped after all."

"I guess not," Dink said. He looked at Ruth Rose. She wasn't smiling.

"There's one thing I don't understand," she finally said. "How did he know who to call? How did that man know who Mozart belonged to?"

Dink shrugged. "Maybe he found him near Mrs. Davis's house and asked one of her neighbors."

"Or," Ruth Rose said, "maybe the guy who called is the same guy who *took* Mozart."

"But that doesn't make sense," Dink said. "Why would someone steal a canary on Thursday and return it the next day?"

"For the reward," Ruth Rose said with a frown. "This guy steals pets, then returns them for money."

Dink and Josh just stared at Ruth Rose.

They walked the rest of the way home in silence.

Chapter 4

Dink and Ruth Rose sat on Dink's front porch. They'd just finished dinner and were waiting for Josh.

Ruth Rose sighed.

"Tiger hasn't come home yet?" Dink asked.

She shook her head.

"Cats can be pretty mysterious sometimes," Dink said. He wanted Ruth Rose to feel better. "Maybe she's visiting a cat buddy somewhere."

Ruth Rose looked down. "She's never stayed away like this."

Suddenly Dink noticed that Ruth Rose had forgotten her headband. Her curly hair was hanging in her eyes.

Just then Josh came running down Woody Street, carrying his sketch pad. He jogged across Dink's lawn.

"Did Tiger come back yet?" he asked.

"No," Ruth Rose said, standing up. "Come on, let's go see who brings Mozart back."

A few minutes later, they were ringing Mrs. Davis's doorbell. Ruth Rose had a determined look in her eye. "If this guy has cat scratches on his hands, I'm calling Officer Fallon."

Mrs. Davis opened her door dressed for the occasion. The green gem in her necklace sparkled in the evening sunlight.

"I hope you've brought your appetites," she said. "To help us celebrate

Mozart's return, I've made some short-cake."

Josh grinned. "I might be able to eat a small helping."

Mrs. Davis laughed. "Oh, pooh, Joshua Pinto. I've seen what you can do to a batch of my cookies."

They walked into the living room. Mozart's empty cage sat on the piano.

"It will be so good to hear Mozart sing again," Mrs. Davis said.

The doorbell chimed. "He's here!" Mrs. Davis hurried to the door.

A thin young man stood smiling on the front porch. He was dressed neatly in a white shirt, dark pants, and blue suspenders.

The man held a small box with holes poked in the sides. "I'm Fred Little," he said. "Here's your canary."

Dink looked at the man's hands as he passed the box to Mrs. Davis. Not a

single claw mark. He shot a look at Ruth Rose.

"Thank you, Mr. Little," said Mrs. Davis. "Won't you step inside?"

Mrs. Davis introduced him to Dink, Josh, and Ruth Rose. Then she opened the box and lifted out her canary.

"Well, Mozart, how was your vacation?" She gave the canary a quick kiss
and placed him in his cage.

Everyone paused to watch Mozart
hop around, then settle down to preen
his feathers.

"Mr. Little, I can't tell you how
grateful I am," Mrs. Davis said. "But
how did you know where to bring
him?"

Ruth Rose kicked Dink in the ankle.

Fred Little smiled. "I had to do some detective work," he said. "I called the pet shop today and asked who in town owned a canary. A nice woman told me your name, so I looked you up in the phone book."

"That must have been Mrs. Wong," Dink said. "We talked to her today, too. About Ruth Rose's missing cat. When did you call her?"

The man stared at Dink. "I don't remember exactly," he said. "It was right after I caught the canary."

Mrs. Davis clapped her hands. "How thoughtful of you to go to so much trouble! Will you accept a reward?"

Ruth Rose glanced at Dink with a smirk on her face.

The man smiled at Mrs. Davis. "You're very kind," he said. "But no thanks. It's reward enough seeing your little bird back home again."

Dink snuck a quick look at Ruth Rose. She looked confused, and Dink could understand why.

If he won't take a reward, then he didn't steal Mozart. And if Mozart didn't get kidnapped, maybe Tiger didn't either, Dink thought.

"Then will you at least have a cup of tea and a cookie?" Mrs. Davis asked.

"That'll be fine," he said. "May I use your bathroom?"

"Down the hall on the right," Mrs. Davis said. "Kids, will you help me in the kitchen?"

While Mrs. Davis boiled water and arranged her silver tea service, the kids put cookies on a tray.

"He didn't take the reward," Ruth Rose whispered, frowning. "I can't believe I was wrong!"

"I don't know, Ruth Rose," Dink said. "There's something fishy about this guy. Why didn't Mrs. Wong tell us he called her?"

"We saw Mrs. Wong in the morning," Josh reminded them. "Fred Little must have called her later."

"Yeah, I suppose," Dink said.

"But I have this weird feeling I've seen Fred Little somewhere before," Josh said.

"Around here?" Ruth Rose asked.

Josh shrugged. "I'm not sure. I can't remember."

"What are you three whispering about?" Mrs. Davis called. "I'll need some helping hands in a minute."

When they were all seated around the card table, Mrs. Davis poured five cups of tea. "Are you just passing through, Mr. Little? I haven't seen you in town before."

"I'm here looking for a job," Fred Little said.

"So you might settle in Green Lawn? Wouldn't that be wonderful!"

Fred Little smiled. "It's a nice town." He glanced around the living room. "You sure have a lovely home, Mrs. Davis."

"Why, thank you. When my husband was alive, we traveled a great deal," Mrs. Davis said. "We brought back something special from each country we visited."

Fred Little left a few minutes later, and the kids helped Mrs. Davis clean up. "Still have room for shortcake?" she asked, grinning at Josh.

"Sure do!" he answered, picking up his sketch pad.

Josh began to draw a picture of Fred Little's face. "I just wish I could remember where I've seen this guy before."

Chapter 5

That night, a thunderstorm sent the kids running from their tents into their houses.

It was still raining the next day, so they decided to play Monopoly at Dink's house.

"Ruth Rose, it's your turn," Josh said.

"I know," she said, staring out Dink's window. "I can't concentrate. Tiger is out there in the rain."

Dink and Josh just looked at each other.

"If Fred Little didn't take the pets, then who could it be?" Ruth Rose asked. She came and plopped herself down at the Monopoly board.

Dink thought a moment. "If we could figure out *why* someone was stealing animals," he said, "maybe we could figure out *who* was doing it."

Ruth Rose picked up her stack of Monopoly cash. "I still think it's for money," she said. "When people get kidnapped, it's usually for ransom money, right?"

The boys nodded.

"But no one who's lost a pet has gotten a ransom note," Josh said.

"Not yet, anyway." Ruth Rose tossed her play money onto the table. "I'm going home. Mom put an ad in the paper, and I want to be there if anyone calls about Tiger."

The two boys watched her put on

her coat and head out into the rain.

"I've never seen her act so mopey," Josh said after the door closed. "She doesn't even argue with me anymore!"

"Yeah, and have you noticed she's not wearing one color either?" Dink pointed out. "I hope Tiger comes home soon."

That night the rain cleared up, so Dink and Josh slept out in the tent again.

The next morning, Ruth Rose woke them up. She was wearing cut-off jeans and an old T-shirt. Her untied sneaker laces were muddy from dragging.

"Read this, guys," she said, and she shoved the *Sunday Morning Gazette* under Dink's nose.

One paragraph was circled in red crayon. Dink and Josh stumbled out of the tent and sat at the picnic table.

The paragraph was under LOCAL

AREA CRIMES. Dink scanned it quickly, then read it out loud:

"Two Green Lawn homes were burglarized last night, Officer Charles Fallon has reported. The homes of Dr. and Mrs. Michael Pardue and Mr. and Mrs. Harvey Gwynn were entered by persons unknown. Several items of value were taken. Police are investigating."

Dink looked up. "Wow! First they lose their pets, then someone breaks into their houses. I think that stinks!"

"And I think they're connected," Ruth Rose said. "Don't you see, it *is* about money! Someone is taking pets, then breaking into the same houses."

"But why would someone need to steal a pet before robbing a house?" Dink asked.

"And not only that," Josh added, "but what about you and Mrs. Davis?

Your pets disappeared, but your houses weren't broken into."

"He's right, Ruth Rose," Dink said. "Why just two houses and not all four?"

Ruth Rose frowned at Dink and Josh. "I don't know," she said.

"We should try and find out. Let's go see the Pardues and the Gwynns again. Maybe the burglars left some clues!"

They hurried over to Thistle Court and rang the bell. Mr. Gwynn came to the door in his bathrobe.

"Oh, hi, kids! Mrs. Gwynn told me you stopped by Friday. Guess what? Yesterday afternoon, someone found our parrot and returned him!"

Ruth Rose stared at Mr. Gwynn. "Archie was returned yesterday?"

Mr. Gwynn nodded. "To celebrate, I took the family out for dinner and a movie. But when we got back home, we

discovered we'd been robbed. The rats took my coin collection."

"I'm sorry to hear that," Dink said.

"May I ask who returned your parrot?"

"A nice young woman," Mr. Gwynn told the kids. "She said she'd caught Archie eating seeds under her bird feeder."

"Did you invite her into your house?" Ruth Rose asked.

Before he could answer, Dink blurted out, "Did she see your coin collection?"

Mr. Gwynn's mouth dropped open. "Are you suggesting...Oh, my, you could be right!" he said. "The collection was in the living room where we sat and talked. Do you think she came back and stole it?"

Dink, Josh, and Ruth Rose looked at one another. Ruth Rose had her "I told you so!" look on her face.

"It sure seems that way, Mr. Gwynn," Dink said.

The kids thanked Mr. Gwynn, then raced all the way to the Pardues' house. Out of breath, Ruth Rose rang the bell.

Mrs. Pardue came to the door. "Hi, gang, what's up?" she said.

Ruth Rose asked, "By any chance, did someone bring your rabbit back yesterday, before your house got robbed?"

"Why, how did you know?" Mrs. Pardue asked. "A nice young couple called and said they'd found Violet in their garden. They brought her home yesterday afternoon."

Dink explained how the Gwynns' parrot had also been returned before they were robbed.

Mrs. Pardue's eyes got wide. "Of course! That couple came in and had a cold drink with us. Dr. Pardue offered them a reward, but they refused it."

"What did they steal?" Josh asked.

"Several pieces of my good jewelry," Mrs. Pardue said. "Some of it was left to me by my grandmother."

Ruth Rose thought for a minute. "Did they ask to use your bathroom?"

"Yes, the woman did," Mrs. Pardue answered. "She could have snooped in my bedroom at the same time. I feel so foolish!"

The kids said good-bye and headed for Main Street.

"I knew it!" Ruth Rose said. "The pet-nappers and the robbers are the same people!"

"Boy, what a dirty scam," Josh said. "You steal someone's pet, return it to get a guided tour of the place, then come back later to take what you liked."

"Talk about a double whammy," Dink said, shaking his head.

"I think it's gonna be a triple whammy," Ruth Rose said. "What about Mrs. Davis?"

"What about her?" Josh asked. "She hasn't...oh, my gosh!"

"That's right," Ruth Rose said. "I'll bet anything that Mrs. Davis's house is next!"

Chapter 6

"Or *your* house could be next," Dink reminded Ruth Rose.

Ruth Rose shook her head. "They didn't return Tiger, so they didn't get inside my house. Come on, we have to tell Officer Fallon!"

They ran down Main Street to the police station.

"Does he work on Sunday morning?" Josh asked as they hurried up the steps.

"We'll find out in a minute," Dink said.

The kids almost bumped into Officer Fallon coming through the door.

"Were you kids coming to see me?" he asked. "I was just heading for Ellie's."

"Officer Fallon, we figured out the burglaries!" Ruth Rose cried.

He looked at her. "Oh? Then we'd better go back inside."

Sitting at his desk, Officer Fallon picked up a pencil. "I'm listening," he said.

Ruth Rose told him their theory about how the pet-nappers came back later to return the animals, then rob the houses.

Officer Fallon smiled. "I think you're right on the button," he said. "I figured out the same thing."

"Did you know that Mrs. Davis's canary was returned, too?" Ruth Rose asked. She looked at Dink and Josh.

"We think *her* house will be robbed next!"

Officer Fallon raised his eyebrows. "Well, now, that *is* news. I didn't know about the canary. When was it returned?" he asked, writing something on his pad.

"Friday night," Josh said. "Some guy called up and said he'd found Mozart. He brought him over while we were there."

Officer Fallon's eyes widened. "Tell me about this man, Josh," he said quietly.

Josh described Fred Little while Officer Fallon took more notes.

"Can you arrest Fred Little before he breaks into Mrs. Davis's house?" Ruth Rose asked.

Officer Fallon tapped his pencil and squinted one eye at the kids. "Officer Keene and I have been looking for whoever returned the Gywnn and Pardue pets. We want to question them about the pet-nappings and the robberies. Now we will start looking for Fred Little, too."

He leaned forward on his elbows. "But we have no evidence that these people have done anything wrong. The same goes for Fred Little. True, he returned the canary and got inside Leona Davis's house. That's the same pattern as the other two burglaries, but it's not a crime."

"You can't arrest him?" Josh asked.

Officer Fallon shook his head. "Even if I knew where to find Fred Little, I have no proof that he's planning a crime."

"But we have to do something!" Ruth Rose said.

"You've already done a lot," Officer Fallon said. "I didn't know that Leona

Davis got her bird back. You've given me a good lead. Officer Keene and I really appreciate your help, kids."

He walked them to the door. "Don't worry, we have a few tricks up our sleeves."

"I still think we should do *something*," Ruth Rose said when they were outside.

"Well..." Josh said. "The circus is leaving tomorrow, and we do have those free tickets Officer Fallon gave us..."

Dink laughed. Together, he and Josh talked Ruth Rose into visiting the circus for a few hours.

They watched a few animal acts and bought popcorn.

Ruth Rose didn't feel like going on any rides, so they decided to go into the clown tent again.

Two clowns dressed as firefighters

were running around, bumping into each other while a small cardboard building "burned."

Smoke and fake flames were shooting out of a window. A woman clown was screaming, "Help! Save me!"

Some of the kids in the audience started yelling, "Save her, mister! Up there, save her!"

The firefighter clowns got tangled up in their own hoses, making everyone laugh and yell even louder.

Suddenly a clown dressed like Superman appeared on stilts. He wore a blue shirt under a red cape. Bright yellow suspenders held up the skinny blue pants that hid his stilts.

Superman flapped his cape and snapped his suspenders. Then he marched over to the burning tower and saved the woman. All the kids in the audience yelled and clapped.

Dink noticed that Ruth Rose was hardly even looking. He nudged Josh, and they left.

"I'd like to get me some stilts," Josh said. He walked stiff-legged and snapped invisible suspenders. "Do circuses ever hire kids?"

"Yeah, to feed to the tigers," Dink said, which reminded him of Ruth Rose's Tiger. He looked at her. "Do you want to come over and finish the Monopoly game?"

She shook her head. "Don't you guys want to solve this mystery?"

"Sure, but what else can we do?" Dink asked. "Officer Fallon said he's

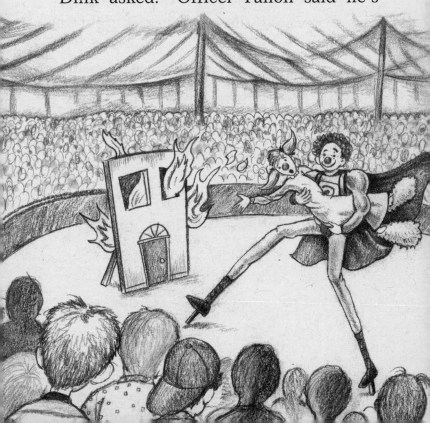

gonna look for the people who returned the pets."

"Well, I know how we can help him," Ruth Rose said, her eyes flashing.

"Uh-oh," Josh mumbled.

"Um, Ruth Rose, I don't think Officer Fallon wants any more help," Dink said.

Ruth Rose ignored him. "Are you guys sleeping in the tent again tonight?" she asked.

Dink nodded. "I guess so. Why?"

Ruth Rose grinned mysteriously. "I promise to bring over some cookies if you promise to go somewhere with me."

"Where?" Dink asked. "And why do you have that sneaky look on your face?"

"Wear dark clothes," Ruth Rose said. "We're going to stake out Mrs. Davis's house!"

Chapter 7

"A stakeout?" Josh said.

Ruth Rose nodded.

"Like in the cop movies?" Dink asked.

She nodded again.

"You think Mrs. Davis's house is going to get robbed tonight?" Josh said.

A third nod. "And I plan to be there to see who does it." She grinned. "Will that be enough proof for Officer Fallon?"

"Suppose a burglar does come," Dink said. "What do we do, tie him up?"

"All right!" Josh said. "I'll bring the rope."

Ruth Rose shook her head. "No rope. We just sit and watch. If someone comes, one of us will run to the police station. The other two will stay. If the guy leaves, we follow him."

Dink thought that over. "Follow him where?"

"Wherever he goes, Dink. Maybe he'll lead us to where he stashed the stuff he robbed," Ruth Rose said. "And maybe that's where he's got Tiger."

"Well, I guess it'll work, as long as we just watch the guy," Dink said.

Ruth Rose nodded. "We just wait and watch."

"And eat cookies," Josh added.

Dink and Josh sat in the dark tent, waiting for Ruth Rose. It was almost ten o'clock.

Josh wore camouflage pants and a black T-shirt. Dink had on jeans and a dark gray sweatshirt.

"Where the heck is she?" Josh asked.

Dink peeked out the tent flap. "My folks will kill me if we get caught running around Green Lawn at night."

"Mine would ground me for ten years," Josh said. "Why'd we let her talk us into this?"

Dink heard a noise. "Did you hear something?" he whispered.

Josh peeked out. "Ruth Rose? Is that you?"

"Boo!" Ruth Rose giggled. "I'm right here, Josh."

Dink poked his head out. He couldn't see a thing. "Come on, Ruth Rose, stop fooling around. Where are you hiding?"

"I'm not hiding!" Suddenly Dink

could see her. Ruth Rose was sitting about four feet away, right in front of him! She was wearing black jeans and a black jacket. Her hair was covered by a ski cap. She'd even blackened her face. Except for the whites of her eyes, Ruth Rose was practically invisible.

"What's that stuff on your face?" Dink asked.

"Liquid shoe polish." She pulled a bottle out of her backpack. "Here, put some on."

"Do we have to?" Dink said.

"Yes! What happens if the burglar sees your two white faces glowing in the moonlight?"

Dink poured some of the polish into his hand and smeared it all over his face. "This stuff stinks," he muttered.

Josh did the same. "I feel like Rambo," he said. Dink saw Josh's white teeth gleaming.

"Let's head out," Ruth Rose said, slipping away from the tent.

The boys followed her down Woody Street. Mrs. Davis's house was dark as they crept into her backyard. Dink tried not to think about what they were doing.

Ruth Rose chose their hiding place, a shadowy patch between two thick bushes behind the house.

The moon was almost full, but large clouds kept slipping in front of it. The kids wiggled around, getting comfortable on the lawn.

"Did you bring the cookies?" Josh asked.

"Yes, but let's save them till later," Ruth Rose said. "We might be here for hours."

Josh let out a big sigh. "People who break their promises..."

"She's right, Josh," Dink whispered.

"And I don't think we should talk anymore. If the burglar comes, he might hear us and take off."

Five seconds passed.

"One little cookie wouldn't kill you, Ruth Rose."

"Josh, this is a stakeout, not Ellie's Diner."

"Cops eat on stakeouts."

"JOSH! SHHH!"

Dink stretched out on the grass. He watched the back of the house for moving shadows. Nothing moved.

He slapped at a mosquito.

A white cat strolled through the yard.

Dink yawned.

Every few minutes, he checked his watch.

He closed his eyes.

When he opened them again, it was nearly eleven o'clock. Josh was sound asleep, but Dink could see that Ruth Rose's eyes were wide open.

"Are you hungry?" she whispered.

He nodded and shook Josh's shoulder.

Ruth Rose opened her pack. She brought out a bag of cookies, three bananas, and three cartons of apple juice.

They ate in silence, listening and watching for a burglar to show up.

"Thanks, Ruth Rose," Josh whispered. Then he lay back down and shut his eyes again.

Dink yawned and tried to get comfortable. He wished he'd brought his sleeping bag. It was soft and...suddenly he saw something move in the shadows next to the house.

He shook Josh and put his mouth next to Ruth Rose's ear. "Look," he whispered, pointing.

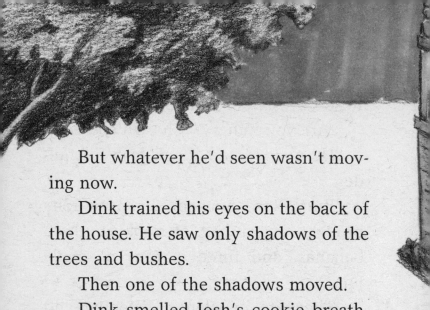

But whatever he'd seen wasn't moving now.

Dink trained his eyes on the back of the house. He saw only shadows of the trees and bushes.

Then one of the shadows moved.

Dink smelled Josh's cookie breath. "He's here!" Josh whispered. Dink could feel Josh trembling with excitement.

Dink's stomach did a quick plunge. Someone dressed in dark clothes and a

baseball cap was creeping behind Mrs. Davis's house. He carried a gym bag and a long pole. The prowler was in the shadows, and Dink couldn't see his face.

The burglar set his bag and the pole on the ground. Then he checked each first-floor window on the back of the house. Finding them all locked, he walked around the side, out of sight.

"What should we do?" Josh said. "Is he leaving?"

Dink shook his head. "He left his stuff."

"Did anyone recognize his face?" Ruth Rose asked.

Nobody had. Suddenly the dark figure returned. He stood with his back to them, looking up at the house.

Then the prowler turned around. He seemed to be looking directly at Dink.

Dink was glad he'd blackened his face. Suddenly Josh grabbed Dink's arm. "It's the canary guy!"

Ruth Rose let out a gasp.

Fred Little was walking right toward them!

Chapter 8

Dink tried to shrink into the dark space between the bushes. He could feel Josh and Ruth Rose doing the same.

His heart thudded as Fred Little stepped closer. Then he stopped, took off his jacket, and hung it on a tree branch three feet from Dink's nose. He walked back toward the house.

Josh grabbed Dink. "Look, he's wearing yellow suspenders!"

Dink remembered where he'd seen those suspenders. He grinned at Josh. "The Superman clown!"

"And the giraffe clown," Josh whispered back. "I *knew* I'd seen him before."

They watched as Fred Little opened his gym bag. He pulled out a coil of rope and looped it around his neck.

Then he picked up the long pole he'd brought with him. Only it wasn't a pole.

Fred Little had brought a pair of long stilts. He carefully leaned the stilts against the house and scooted up the foot rests. Now about ten feet tall, he stilt-walked to a spot under a small window on the second floor.

A moment later, Dink watched Fred Little slip through the window. First he was standing there on stilts, and then he was gone, like a snake slithering into a hole.

The stilts remained leaning against the side of the house.

Josh was at Dink's ear. "Should we—"

"Shhh, wait," Ruth Rose whispered.

Suddenly the rope uncoiled from the window. One end dangled to the ground, between the stilts.

"That must be how he's coming down," Ruth Rose said.

"Let's take the rope and stilts," Josh whispered. "He'll be trapped inside!"

"But Mrs. Davis is in there with him," Ruth Rose said. "We have to let him come out, then follow him."

"One of us should run to the police station now," Dink said.

The trouble was, no one wanted to leave the excitement.

Suddenly three things happened at once: The upstairs light blazed on. Dink heard a loud scream. A police whistle blared through the open window.

Dink leaped to his feet, not sure

what to do. Mrs. Davis was up there, and the burglar was probably in the same room with her!

But which one had let out that scream?

Dink saw a silhouette appear at the window. A second later, Fred Little was climbing down his escape rope. With his feet still above the ground, he dropped.

Suddenly the backyard exploded in color and noise.

A police cruiser roared across Mrs. Davis's lawn, flashing red, yellow, and blue lights. The backyard looked like a fireworks display.

The siren whooped loudly, shutting out the shrieking of the whistle.

Then the noise stopped as the cruiser doors burst open. Officers Fallon and Keene leaped out.

"Hold it!" Officer Fallon shouted.

Fred Little was still crouched on the ground where he had landed. Dink saw his mouth fall open in panic and surprise.

In seconds, he was wearing handcuffs.

As Officer Keene led the prisoner to the police car, the back door flew open. Mrs. Davis marched out in a white nightgown and floppy slippers. She flip-flopped across the yard toward Fred Little.

Her face was shiny with white cream. Some kind of lacy bonnet covered her hair. And she held a long sword high over her head.

"The nerve of you!" she yelled into Fred Little's terrified face. "Coming right into my bedroom!"

The sword flashed in the cruiser's headlights. Dink thought she was going to use it on the burglar!

"I heard you trying to find my jewelry!" she shouted. "And after I fed you tea and cookies!"

"Come on," Ruth Rose said.

Everyone, but especially Fred Little, was surprised to see three little ninjas crawl out of the bushes.

Chapter 9

Ruth Rose stomped up to Fred Little and glared at him. "Where's my Tiger?" she demanded.

Fred Little backed away. "What tiger?"

"Tiger is my cat. Did you steal her? Where is she?"

"I didn't take any cat," he muttered. "I'm allergic to cats."

"What're you kids doing here?" Officer Fallon asked with a frown.

"We thought someone might try to break in tonight," Ruth Rose said, pointing at the prisoner. "We wanted to get proof so you could arrest him."

"This is Fred Little," Josh said. "The guy who returned Mrs. Davis's canary. He's also a clown in the circus."

"And he's probably the one who robbed Dr. Pardue's house and the Gwynns', too," Dink added.

"It certainly looks that way," Officer Fallon said. He gave instructions to Officer Keene, who locked Fred Little in the cruiser and drove away.

Officer Fallon looked sternly at Dink. "We'll talk tomorrow," he said. "You kids better skedaddle home and get some sleep."

"Fiddlesticks!" Mrs. Davis said. "These children won't perish if they stay up a little longer. And *I* won't sleep a wink! Come inside for cookies and cocoa, all of you."

Officer Fallon just smiled and shook his head as they followed Mrs. Davis into her kitchen. Dink noticed Mozart's cage sitting on the counter.

Mrs. Davis put water on to boil and took mugs from a cupboard. Then she pulled the cover off the birdcage. Mozart twittered and blinked his tiny black eyes.

"You've certainly put everyone through a lot of trouble," she told her canary.

"Actually, Leona, your canary helped us to solve a string of burglaries," Officer Fallon said. "I did some snooping and found out a lot about Fred Little and his girlfriend. They've been traveling with the circus, and robbing houses in the towns they visit, for quite some time. And they always do it the same way. First they steal pets. Then they return the pets to get a peek inside the houses. Later, they rob the same houses."

Mrs. Davis shook her head. "You should have seen that creepy man's face when I turned on the light. But how did he know I left my upstairs bathroom window open?"

"He probably saw that it was open when he took your canary," Officer Fallon said.

"Or maybe he left it open," Dink said. "He might have snuck upstairs when he used the bathroom."

"You could be right, Dink," Officer Fallon said. "On stilts, he could get into upstairs windows that most people leave unlocked. In the robbery business, he's known as a second-story man."

"After tonight," Mrs. Davis said, "that window will be locked!"

"How did you know that Fred Little would try to break in tonight?" Dink asked.

"We were parked right around the corner," Officer Fallon continued. "We figured the burglary had to be tonight or never, since the circus leaves town tomorrow."

Suddenly there was a knock at the door. Officer Fallon stood up and stretched. "That'll be Officer Keene back with the car. We'll drive you kids home now. I hope we didn't wreck your yard, Leona."

"Oh, pooh. You saved my jewelry and caught a pair of criminals," she said. "Besides, I know three children who might like to earn some money raking and planting grass seed."

Officer Fallon laughed. "You could have caught Fred Little all by yourself. Where'd that sword come from, Leona?"

"My husband brought it back from one of our trips," she said, smiling. "It's been under my bed for years, in case I ever needed it."

"Did you see that guy's face?" Josh asked. "I think he was glad to go to jail!"

Officer Fallon and Officer Keene dropped the kids off at Dink's house. "Good night, kids," Officer Fallon said. "No more sneaking around, okay?"

The kids promised they'd go right to bed and watched the cruiser drive away.

"I wonder if Fred Little was telling the truth about Tiger," Ruth Rose said. "All the pets got returned except mine."

"Tomorrow we'll help you search, right, Josh?" Dink said.

"Right," Josh said. "We'll ring every doorbell in Green Lawn if we have to."

Ruth Rose nodded, looking sad. "Thanks, guys."

The boys said good night to Ruth

Rose, then walked around back and crawled into their tent.

Josh giggled in the dark. "Did you see Mrs. Davis come flying out her door with all that goop on her face? I thought she was a ghost!"

Dink grinned. "Yeah, and old Fred Little came shooting out the window like a rocket. I bet he burned his hands sliding down that rope."

Dink rolled over and closed his eyes.

Thirty seconds later, Ruth Rose burst through the tent flap. She shined a flashlight into Dink's face.

"GUYS, WAKE UP!" she yelled.

Josh bolted straight up. "Geez, Ruth Rose, my heart can't take any more surprises tonight."

"What's wrong?" Dink asked, blinking.

"TIGER CAME HOME!" Ruth Rose

said, flopping down next to Dink's feet. "She was on my bed when I snuck upstairs. When I went to pick her up, she hopped down and crawled under the bed."

Ruth Rose grinned. "And guess what I found under there with her?"

"A sword?" Dink guessed.

"Nope!"

"A burglar?" Josh asked, blinking into the flashlight.

"No! I found three kittens. I'M A GRANDMOTHER!"

A to Z Mysteries™

Dear Readers,

When I was in fifth grade, I bought a parakeet and named him Buddy. I tried to teach him to say his name, but Buddy only spoke in parakeet language. One day, my brother let Buddy out of his cage. Buddy disappeared fast! I searched and searched, but couldn't find him anywhere. Just when I didn't know where else to look, I heard a voice say "Buddy" from behind the living room drapes.

Recently, I stopped to look at birds in a pet shop window. I thought about Buddy, my parakeet. That was the day I began to plan *The Canary Caper*. I hope Buddy would be pleased with the book!

I get my ideas from many places: from what I read, from what I dream, from what friends tell me. But I also get a lot of ideas from my readers, so I hope you'll write to me. Please send your letters to:

Ron Roy
c/o Random House
Children's Books
1540 Broadway, 19th floor
New York, NY 10036

Happy reading!

Best regards,

Ron Roy

Collect clues with Dink, Josh, and Ruth Rose
in their next exciting adventure,

THE DEADLY DUNGEON!

Dink and Ruth Rose followed Josh. The cave grew darker, until the sunlight had completely disappeared. The air was cold and damp, and the black walls looked slimy.

"Josh, this water is freezing," Ruth Rose said. Her voice sounded hollow. "I hate it in here! Can we go back?"

"The water's getting deeper, too," Dink said. "And I can't even see you guys!"

"Shh!" Josh said. "I heard something!"

"Josh, don't try to scare us!" Ruth Rose said. "I'm already—"

Suddenly a scream echoed off the cave walls.

"RUN!" Ruth Rose yelled.